# Captain Kangaroo and the Great Balloon Race

Illustrated by
## Mandy Foot

LOTHIAN
Children's Books

D1422167

For brilliant books, fun and games visit
# www.mandyfoot.com.au

For Joshy,
for all grandparents,
and for all the little ones …
may your dreams fly high like the great big balloons!

A Lothian Children's Book

Published in Australia and New Zealand in 2012
by Hachette Australia
Level 17, 207 Kent Street, Sydney NSW 2000
www.hachettechildrens.com.au

10 9 8 7 6 5 4 3

National Library of Australia
Cataloguing-in-Publication data

Mandy Foot.
Captain Kangaroo and the Great Balloon Race / Mandy Foot.

978 0 7344 1267 6 (hbk.)
978 0 7344 1265 2 (pbk.)

For children.

A823.4

Designed by Kinart Pty Ltd
Colour reproduction by Splitting Image
Printed in China by Toppan Leefung Printing Limited

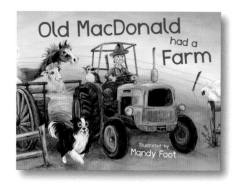

Can you find the hidden animal in each race picture?
The clue is on the last page!

Captain Kangaroo sets the gears for landing
but now he's spotted trouble.
Why is the runway hidden by
a cloud of coloured bubbles?

The captain lands safely in a paddock
and hops back without delay.

The Great Balloon Race is starting!

He waves the flag to CHEER them on their way.

The wombats slap on sunscreen, as the hot sun GLOWS and glares.
The echidnas see the holes they've made – too late to make repairs!

Whoops! A koala pulls away a safety rope as he dreams and dozes.
A bossy ring-tail almost tumbles out, but holds on by a nose.

Suddenly, the wind changes direction, and the emus *SAIL* ahead.

They're the first to notice that the sky has changed from blue to red.

Now there *really* might be trouble,
so they call Captain Kangaroo.

With his fleet of rescue aircraft
he'll know exactly what to do.

The entire competition drifts
inside the **giant** cloud.
The balloons are bumping left and right,
the wind is whistling loud.

The Captain sets the blades to overdrive
as his helicopter nears.
He SWIRLS and WHIRLS the dust
till it completely disappears.

When the sea begins to settle,
the baskets drop and BOB ABOUT.
The captain releases safety ropes
and hauls each contestant out.

The animals SQUASH inside the chopper
– all tangled wings and legs.
The pelican pokes the wombat,
the koalas grab the emus' necks.

The captain hands everyone a **ribbon.**
'You've been as brave as brave can be!
Now, my next flight is due for take-off.
Who'd like to come with me?'

Would *you* like to fly too with Captain Kangaroo?